The Power of My Scars

A Short Story Based on True Events

By

Jennifer Garfinkel

Disclaimer

Fictional names have been used in the story to protect the privacy of individuals.

Table of Contents

Acknowledgments

A HUGE thank you to my family members and friends for all that they have done for me during my trauma and healing.

The endless amounts of time they spent with me during the tiresome days in the hospital and rehab is something I will never forget.

Words and actions cannot express how deeply gracious I am to have you in my life. From the conversations I have had, to the small gestures it will never be forgotten.

I would also like to thank all the people who pushed me to believe that life will get better. You brought me out of my funk when I should not have been in one in the first place.

I want to thank the people who got me out of the house, invited me to go somewhere, and distracted me from everything going on in my head.

To my supervisor Gianna, and coworker Katherine, who pushed me to do something I really did not want to do. THANK YOU! You might have saved my life. I am truly grateful for that.

THANK YOU! To my work family who did everything they could to cheer me up. The random texts and cards that were sent to me genuinely mean a lot.

To the doctors and nurses in the hospital that were able to diagnose my problem - it was hard to crack, but you did it. I guess that is why you all went through years of medical school!

To the rehab team in the hospital - you are AMAZING! You brought me back to life as if I were a comatose patient and that is something I will never forget.

And finally, to the man that I loved too much when I shouldn't have. You unexpectedly came into my life and treated me like a princess. I want to thank you for being a part of my life and showing me what I deserve. Whether it was fake or not, the time we spent together was precious to me and taught me so much. THANK YOU!

Introduction

This is a short story that I wrote when I was broken and vulnerable.

I would imagine that is how many short stories get made from personal experiences. My perfect life was torn apart and turned upside down.

The journey was long and difficult to say the least. I lost something and someone I loved very much. Probably too much. All I have left are scars and memories. Both good and bad.

I know it is only a chapter of my life, but it is a horrible one.

My short story is based on true events that happened in such a short period of time.

It is a story about acceptance and determination. The hand we are dealt with is not always the one we want to play and yet we must learn how to keep playing it.

Life happens before we are ready for it sometimes. It has its ups and downs and lefts and rights.

Curveballs get thrown at us and it is about how we deal with those curveballs. Do we watch the curveball pass us, or do we hit it in hopes that it turns into a home run? Only you can answer that question.

This short story is about pain and overcoming adversity and whatever else life decides to surprisingly throw at us. The heartache of having to move on when you just want to hold tight to your life.

I unfortunately had to let go of what I thought was going to be my perfect life.

Letting go is a process and does not come easy.

This is for everybody who is going through tough times. It gets better. Believe me. I hit rock bottom and turned my life around. I was fighting a battle I never thought would end all on my own.

I hope that some part, if not all, of this story will help you in your process, wherever that might be.

Chapter 1 – Covid-19

It all started on a sunny, warm winter day in January—January 15th to be exact. I will never forget this day. I had the perfect life. A great job, an incredible boyfriend, and an amazing place to call home. However, on this day my world started to fall apart piece by piece, and soon, it completely shattered!!

I contracted Covid-19 two weeks prior when I was in New York City to celebrate New Year's Eve with the love of my life. It also happened to be his birthday! Well, I at least thought he was the love of my life, which I will explain in a later chapter.

It was the first time the both of us had spent the holiday in the BIG APPLE overnight. It was exciting—a night I think we both will never forget!

I am not sure how I got sick and I guess I will never know. Was it from my boyfriend Javier, who was sick the day before? Who knows.

This is now the second time I have had Covid. Maybe it is because I had gotten the vaccine and booster shots a few times. However, it was just a bad cold for me.

I know it affects everyone differently, but I am a very healthy person with no underlying issues except for something very rare that happened to me as a child that is also a mystery.

After 10 days of being home isolated and mostly symptom-free, I was allowed to return to work per CDC rules and my company's policy with a mask on. I could not wait to return! I was anxious.

On this day, I was starting to feel a bit better and getting back to my old self. I unfortunately had lost ten pounds from not eating for two weeks, but I was mostly back to normal.

Suddenly, at 1:15 in the afternoon, I was sitting at work in my cubicle staring at the computer screen, and got very confused. My coworker Katherine, called me in the middle of all of this. I explained to her on the phone that I was having a hard time figuring out what to do next and couldn't understand why.

Katherine advised me to talk to my supervisor Gianna. Of course I ignored her suggestion. As a result of having lost a lot of weight and not eating right, I thought maybe I was getting a migraine and could remedy it by simply having something small to eat.

Seconds later, I decided to go for a lunch break. I ate a little bit and got some fresh air, and before you knew it, an hour had passed and I started to feel a little better.

Once I came back from my lunch break everything went downhill. Shortly after the break, I started to lose sensation in my left arm. And then it was my left leg. I was terrified. I couldn't move at all!! I was panicking!!

What was happening? I didn't know what to do. Should I tell someone near me? Do I call 911? My boyfriend? I did none of those things. I did not want to disrupt anyone around me while they were working. I also didn't want to leave work. I just sat there in a daze for a few minutes trying to think clearly, but I couldn't. I was in panic mode!

Moments later, I somehow managed to get up from my cubicle to walk over to my supervisor's office. I explained to her what was happening and how I was feeling. Something was certainly wrong with me. I felt "off," I told her.

I was barely able to walk and was having issues trying to say what I wanted. She looked concerned and advised me to call my doctor.

My coworker Katherine, who was in Gianna's office at the time, followed me back to my cubicle. She walked behind me, studying my behavior as I walked slowly back to where I was sitting. Katherine was worried and concerned. She saw that the left side of my face had a droop in it as I was talking to her. She was talking to me, but I could barely understand her. Everything was cloudy and unclear.

Katherine stood over me and waited for me to call the doctor. She was persistent and wouldn't leave my side until I did it.

I remember the phone just ringing and ringing. The seconds it took for a nurse to pick up felt like a lifetime!

I was finally able to speak with a nurse who advised me to go to the ER and I followed her advice. Since I was unable to really move at this point, I called my elderly parents because I did not want to trouble my coworkers or anyone else.

I called them and explained what was happening. They were nervous and weren't sure what to say or think. Without hesitation, they immediately jumped in the car and in what seemed like only a few moments, were at my office to pick me up and take me to the emergency room.

Chapter 2 – The Diagnosis

Forty-five minutes later, I was in the emergency room at the hospital. Upon entry into the hospital, I was rushed to a wheelchair because I could not walk too well. I was then asked nearly a dozen questions by the triage nurses. Unfortunately, I could not talk very well either because I still had drooping in my face that never seemed to want to go away. The nurses took my blood pressure and temperature and gave me aspirin. Several hours later, I was given a room in the emergency department. I was nervous! The hospital thought I was having a heart attack, but it did not feel like one.

They ran every test imaginable on me. A CT scan of my head, numerous amounts of bloodwork, and several tests on my heart.

What was going on? Why couldn't anyone find an answer for me? Everything was coming back negative and I was still feeling "numb." I was impatient. I needed to know what was going on for the sake of my sanity.

You watch all these doctor shows on TV and they have all the answers just like that. I was hoping that's what my situation would be, but it wasn't that simple. I was poked and prodded at continuously.

Finally, after hours of tests, bloodwork, and no solution, there was only one thing left to do.

The nurses and doctors told me that an MRI of my head had to be done, but because I entered the ER so late, the technician left for the day. They went on to tell me that if I stayed overnight I would be sure to get in first thing in the morning.

Maybe the MRI would give me the answer I needed.

I was hesitant to stay. I disliked hospitals let alone staying in them. Who doesn't? With some reluctance and persuasion by my parents I decided to stay in the ER that night and struggled to get any sleep. The lights were so bright and the constant alarms were so loud. It was miserable!

The next morning came. It was January 16th. I was admitted to a room. FINALLY!

I was feeling a tad bit better. Probably because of all the medication they had given me, but I still couldn't walk or move. It was the strangest feeling. I also didn't have any sensation in my left hand.

When was I going for that MRI? I thought. Many nurses came and went. Many doctors came and went. Seconds passed, minutes passed, hours passed. I was impatient. I needed to get this test done to get an answer and return to work. I was in denial and would text Katherine and Gianna to tell them I would be back to work the next day.

What was the holdup? I was persuaded to stay but never got the MRI done. I asked my nurse what the hold up was and she just said she would check. Of course she never came back to tell me what was going on. Nothing! No answers! I was furious at this point. I felt like I had been lied to. I just kept telling myself, "today is the day!"

That day went by. Long boring hours spent in the hospital and FINALLY, on January 18th, I was able to go for the MRI. IT WAS A MIRACLE! I had spent three days in this crappy, smelly place and had been extremely irritable, restless, anxious, and bored!!

The results took a while to come back. Of course, they did! What hospital does give quick answers? Eventually the doctors came in to tell me the results.

It was an intense STROKE! An ISCHEMIC STROKE that left me paralyzed both physically and mentally all on my left side.

WHAT?!? I could hardly believe my ears! Did I hear that right? Do they have the correct chart? Did they walk into the correct room?

I was in disbelief. ME? A 37-year-old very healthy and active female? That could not be possible!! I was in denial and convinced they were wrong.

I guess it all made sense, but I would have never imagined that this would have been my diagnosis.

I cried my eyes out for hours. My life flashed before me as if I were an older person who was about to die. What am I going to do? I was stunned in all ways possible. This is horrible!! Will I ever be my old self again? This is very scary s**t!!!

Once I received a diagnosis that morning, I saw a team of trained therapists. An Occupational Therapist, a Physical Therapist, and a Speech Therapist. They all tried to help me get back to my normal self. I spent days in a hospital bed. My bones and muscles all felt so dead inside.

With pain and suffering, I was slowly getting the sensation back in my bones, but I was still not myself. It was almost like everything in my body had to be woken up again from a deep sleep. I had to learn how to walk again and move around. Just like a toddler, but I was determined!

Ultimately, after two days of the therapy sessions, the hospital couldn't do anything else for me. They recommended me to a rehab facility as the next step in my healing process, where I would get a higher level of care. It was a bittersweet moment for me. I was happy to leave the smelly hospital, which was my "home" for four days, but sad I wasn't going to my real home.

The evening of January 18th was when I was leaving the hospital and entering my rehab facility. It was a very cold winter day that I will never forget.

I was in rehab for a total of fourteen LONG days. It was rough! I was depressed most of the time and always upset. I would put on a fake happy face for everyone so they wouldn't ask me questions or think otherwise.

During my time in the hospital and in rehab, I was also still emaciated looking. I had a nutritionist who would check on me at least twice a day to make sure I had everything I needed. She recommended I drink a shake twice a day to regain my strength and energy back. It was gross, but I took the necessary steps to get back to normal.

The rehab facility also didn't have great meals to choose from. I would have my family members and friends bring me outside food to eat. I was forcing myself to eat at this point. What other choice did I have?

My treatment plan for walking and movement on my left side included three hours of INTENSE therapy daily Monday through Friday, and on the weekends. I wasn't sure that the three hours a day was going to cut it for my prognosis. I wanted more time with my physical therapists to be ME again.

When I wasn't in my therapy sessions, my family and friends came to visit once they heard the news.

When no one was around, I would cry myself to sleep. *Would I ever get back to normal?* I thought. Even just writing this now is making me emotional. The recovery was tough!!

The days in rehab were a battle. I used a walker to move around wherever I had to go, I had to relearn how to dress myself, my meals had to be cut up like I was a child, and when I wanted to shower (which was every other day), I had to use a shower chair. I always had to call an aide when I wanted to use the bathroom as well. It was terrible!!

I felt like I was in a jail that I would never get out of. My independence and freedom vanished!! I wasn't used to this lifestyle at all. Everything seemed foreign to me.

I met a lot of people during the time I spent in rehab. There was a wide range of people of all different ages. This included doctors, nurses, aides, and therapists. I even had older roommates that were in worse shape than I was. In a lot of ways, these were the people who gave me my willpower, strength, and determination to feel better and be better.

They were all very friendly, but I was still aching to go back to my old life. "When will that be?" I would say to myself. I was hopeful that it would be soon and was always counting down the days. The time couldn't go by fast enough!!

After an intense amount of therapy and finally getting most of the feeling back in my left side, I was able to go home on January 31st. There was nothing left for rehab to do for me. It was all up to me! HALLELUJAH!!

The doctors and staff had to have a meeting about when I was allowed to leave. It wasn't that easy to escape without permission! Lots of paperwork was drawn up for me to sign and instructions on what to do next according to my outpatient treatment and exercises. They all met to discuss which day would be best for me to go home based on the progress I had made during my time spent there.

However, "home" would temporarily be at my parent's house, not my cooperative. I had missed out on many life events while I was in the hospital and rehab, including a holiday party, a New York Islanders game, and a birthday party. I was looking forward to all those events. Yet, being anywhere that was not a hospital or rehab center would be ok with me. I was beyond excited to be free!!

Once the intense therapy was over in the rehab center, I was recommended an outpatient program for more therapy. This was very tiresome and never-ending.

The program consisted of Speech, Occupational Therapy, and Physical Therapy services again. During the outpatient services, I was still unable to drive and go to work. I had to rely on others to drive me around which was not fun at all. I missed my freedom, but I made sure that that would change very quickly.

Life was ultimately looking up for me again, but it was still not easy. I started working part-time while simultaneously going to my therapy sessions.

Getting back to normal took a lot out of me both physically and emotionally. It was very weird after a month and a half. Working and attending therapy was not the best scenario either, but at the time, I would take anything I could get. I was proud of where I was heading and continued to keep going.

After several weeks of exercise and lots of practice, I was pretty much back to normal again. My depression faded and I started to feel happy again. I was able to drive and move back home to MY place.

I had missed almost two months of work and couldn't wait to go back! Crazy, I know. It's the little things in life that mean the most to me.

I felt like I had missed out on so much. I missed my old life so much and was determined to get it back. My life was slowly getting back to normal. I was in such a bad place mentally when this all started.

Chapter 3 – The Breakup

I have been dreading this chapter. I have done everything in my power not to face this part of my trauma and I can honestly say that I've done a great job of not talking about it. At least out loud.

I guess writing about it is a part of the healing process. Right? I never thought I would be able to talk about it. I hate having to think about this part of my life. It is one of the most devastating times of my life and gets me emotional every single time.

I started talking to Javier Albino in the beginning half of 2023. We met unexpectedly on a dating website and started talking immediately. Our chemistry was undeniable. I didn't think it was going to go beyond talking for a few days.

Javier was kind, generous, sweet, handsome, funny, and to me, an all-around nice guy. He was the kind of guy that would always initiate everything first. The first kiss, the conversations, the texts, etc. Everything I wanted in a potential boyfriend and future husband.

He made all the effort in our relationship. Everything just clicked and was effortless! Javier made me believe that I was special to him. He also made me think that we were going to have a future together.

We spent a lot of time together, which I thought was very odd. Everything was perfect during our time together. Even our first date lasted 7 hours. Never in my life has that ever happened before. Our connection was unique and electrifying! Almost too good to be true.

We were inseparable. Always talking or texting one another. Was he really into me that much? I met his family and friends. He met mine. We spent the holidays together. We even went on vacation together. Everything a normal couple would do.

He would mention moving in, getting married, and having kids. WOW! Is he serious? I wasn't even thinking of these things. Things were moving in the right direction and at a fast pace. I was reluctant but fell for Javier very quickly! It was fate. He was my best friend and meant everything to me in such a short period of time.

This is too good to be true I thought to myself. How could such an amazing man care about me so much?!? How could he be so perfect for me? Am I in a dream? I had my doubts but ignored them because I thought they weren't important. I was ready to start the rest of my life with this man and I was extremely excited about it!

Suddenly, on the day I went to the hospital Javier texted me and said, "I hope you got home safely." I didn't know what to say back. I was scared. What should I do? Should I ignore the text? Do I tell him where I am? I decided to answer him and be honest. After all, I did think he deserved to know the truth.

I told him I was in the emergency room and tests were being run on me. He showed concern and asked some questions, but I unfortunately had no answers for him.

Throughout my days in the hospital, Javier wasn't texting me much. Something was going on, but what? He would text me here and there and ask questions about my health, but I sensed something was different. Oddly enough I was reaching out to him all the time. I was grasping at straws. Why was he being so distant? What did I do? You would think that after spending so much time together, he would care enough to call me or see me, right? Did he not believe what was going on? I was beside myself. I knew that focusing on me was more important at the time, but I needed to know what was going on with him.

Once I found out my diagnosis, I texted Javier to tell him. I assumed he was an important part of my life so I should tell him, right? I thought maybe he would come to the rehab center with flowers or text me or my family to see how I was doing. I wanted him with me at the hospital and rehab, but he was MIA and never came. I was aching to see the man of my dreams.

I was shaking as I was texting him. What will he think when I tell him? Will he be more concerned? I was hoping that was the case.

I told Javier the truth about what happened once I found out. I wanted to be honest with him.

Once I told him he became very distant. Why? Did I make a mistake in telling him? He probably would have found out sooner or later if I hadn't told him. Or would he? He acted like he didn't care and that crushed me. I was in disbelief. The man who would text me every day to say that he loved me so much was now a stranger and someone I did not recognize at all.

It took Javier 5 days to break up with me and he did it over a text message!! Not even a lousy phone call!! What kind of a man does that?

The text message was so cold. He was not the man I thought I knew either. It said, "I think we should focus on ourselves. I'm sorry this happened."

Out of all the times to break up with someone, why do it now? I just suffered a life-altering medical issue and this is your response to me?

WHAT ARE YOU THINKING? WOW! I was heartbroken and blindsided. Way to kick someone while they are already down on the ground. What a selfish jerk!!

I pleaded with him over text messages to not end things. We had been through so much together.

So many amazing memories and never once did we have a major fight. I was determined to make things right. I was so in love with him that I begged him to stay even though I knew he had already given up on us. Did he not care about me anymore?

I had gone through so much in the last few days that I needed him now more than ever. I never thought this would happen. There was nothing I could do to change his mind.

He was sticking to his decision and that was final. I felt so alone. How could he be so cruel and heartless during this horrific time of my life? Needless to say, that was the last time I heard from Javier.

Chapter 4 – Everyday Life

It has been almost a year since my life was shattered and ripped apart from me. I still get extremely emotional thinking about it. I know a time will come when it will be just a distant memory and everything will hopefully be easier.

I had to pick up the pieces and rebuild my life little by little. I have scars. Emotional scars that I don't think time will ever heal.

The past never goes away. If you don't deny it, you learn from it. This year has taught me that anybody can change suddenly and anything can happen at any time. One bad chapter does not mean your story is over. All you have to do is turn the page and start over.

These past few months have taught me so much about myself and a part of me wants to thank Javier for it. The heartbreak hurt like hell, but it taught me what I need or want from a significant other. After all, he did say we should focus on ourselves.

By the end of this year, I want to look back at my first half and say, "Damn, I really did believe in myself and worked hard."

Javier was charming and he used his charm to pull me in and win me over. He did an amazing job of it too. He was a good actor and fooled everyone I know. He knew all the right things to say and do. It was almost like he read books on it. But why? Why did he waste my time and his? What was his gain? Was it to fill a void? Did he want to be loved by me? Because that is all I did.

I loved him unconditionally. He was everything to me at one point in time and I did everything in my power to keep our relationship until I couldn't.

My future with him was so close I could taste it, or at least I thought so. We went from lovers to complete strangers in a matter of a few days. He gave up way too easily on our relationship. He just completely blocked me from his life in all ways possible. Like I never existed. He broke me mentally and emotionally. That is a hard pill to swallow.

I have so many unanswered questions about my relationship with Javier. Some of them are:

Why did he break up with me?

Was I not "perfect" to him anymore?

If I didn't have a stroke, would we still be together?

Did he ever really care about me, or was he just using me?

Will I ever hear or see him again?

Our story was never meant to end, or was it?

I so badly want to reach out to him, but I know I shouldn't. He was a huge part of my life. I dedicated so much of my time and energy to a man who I thought was going to be "my forever." Looking back, I feel so ridiculous for fighting for someone who was ok with losing me.

The other questions I have unanswered are related to my stroke. Some of them are:

Will anyone ever know why this happened?

Was it to teach me a lesson?

To this day, the doctors do not have any answers for me. They just say that what happened to me was rare and unheard of for someone my age.

Apparently, having a stroke is not uncommon. It can happen to anyone at any age. I am not sure what triggered mine. Maybe a combination of COVID, stress, extreme weight loss, and everything that went on with Javier.

I'm not 100% sure, but I do not wish what happened to me on anyone else. I was fighting an emotional and mental battle all on my own, which I do not wish on anyone. It felt like it would never end!

Ever since I got out of rehab in January, I have been determined. I was determined to get back on my feet and walk again. I was determined to gain sensation in my hand again and I did just that.

I set mini goals for myself every day and succeeded. I am extremely proud of myself for who I am today. I believed in myself.

I have gone through all the many stages of this short journey. The shock and disbelief. The denial. The anger. The hurt. The acceptance and finally, the face your feelings stage.

I had to keep walking through the storm to get to the rainbow that was waiting on the other side for me. I dug myself out of a very deep hole that I should not have been in in the first place.

Life has been a bit of a struggle these last few months and I don't think I will ever fully recover to who I was before. I have had no choice but to accept what has happened with my stroke, my horrible breakup, and what life threw at me suddenly.

I have been kicked down by what has been thrown at me in life, but I keep getting back up and pushing through.

My life was incredibly hard at the beginning of this year. I had to navigate it in a new way after all the trauma and pain I endured in such a short period of time. My job now is to focus on the music and change the song repeatedly.

I have written Javier an email as a form of closure for myself, but I never heard back from him and I doubt I ever will.

He will always hold a special place in my heart, but I will now remember him as a selfish human being.

In a strange way, the breakup saved me from what could have been.

I guess I am better off without him since I didn't mean anything to him. I wish him nothing but the best and I will never forget how he treated me when I needed his support the most.

As far as my recovery goes, I'm 99% ME again.

I have surrounded myself with positivity and have joined yoga, kickboxing, and boxing classes. This is my way of de-stressing from life or when things get tough and I am ready to burst into tears. I am also constantly busy doing other things so I don't have to stop and think of my shattered life in the beginning half of this year. It was an absolute nightmare for me and especially my family!

This was all just an awful chapter of my life and it is time to keep moving forward! It was a lesson and an experience all at once.

Life goes on, right?

I hope someday I will understand why things happened the way they did and why they were all part of guiding me to where I was meant to be.

To anyone who is struggling out there, just know that it gets better. Life has a way of throwing obstacles at you to see how you can handle it. If you are down in the dumps, you can only move in one direction, and that's UP! There are brighter days ahead!!

Always remember that you can have the worst days of your life, and a few weeks later, you can have the best days of your life. Keep pushing through!

Things happen in life that don't make sense. As you navigate your way through it, it becomes clear that nothing is out of the realm of possibilities. While you can't control what life throws at you, you can control how you rebuild and rise above the moments that turn your world upside down. There is good and bad in life, and you can't let the bad hold power over the good. Sometimes, you need to push through the tough times to truly appreciate the good ones.

Every day you have a choice. You can focus on all the many reasons why you shouldn't be angry and sad, or you can focus on all the many reasons why you should be happy and grateful. Choose wisely!

www.ingramcontent.com/pod-product-compliance
Lightning Source LLC
Chambersburg PA
CBHW060957120626
46557CB00003B/1197